This book belongs to

Brittainy Heitzman

Published by Allen D. Bragdon Publishers, Inc.
153 West 82nd Street, New York, N.Y. 10024

Originally published by M.A. Donahue & Company

Distributed to the book trade in the U.S. and Canada
by Kampmann & Company, 9 E. 40th St., NYC 10016

Manufactured in Hong Kong 1 2 3 4 5 6 7 8 9 10

Library of Congress Cataloging in Publication Data

Little Red Riding-Hood.

Facsim. of: New York : Donahue, 1925.
Summary: A little girl meets a hungry wolf in the
forest while on her way to visit her grandmother.
[1. Fairy tales. 2. Folklore—France] I. Perrault,
Charles, 1628–1703. Petit Chaperon rouge.
PZ8.1.733 1986 398.2'1'0944 86–11772
ISBN 0-916410-35-8

LITTLE RED
RIDING-HOOD

(RETOLD)

COLORED
ILLUSTRATIONS

Allen D. Bragdon Publishers, Inc.

Little Red Riding-Hood

(Retold)

ONCE upon a time, there lived a little girl whose grandmother was so fond of her that she made her a little red cloak and hood. The little girl looked so happy when she wore it that everyone called her "Little Red Riding-Hood."

LITTLE RED RIDING-HOOD

ONE day Little Red Riding-Hood's mother said to her, "You may go to see grandmother today, and, as the air is cool, you may wear your beautiful new cloak"—

THEN she gave her a basket, covered with a snowy napkin. "Here are butter and eggs," she said, "And a little honey for dear grandmother, who is ill.

LITTLE RED RIDING-HOOD

TAKE the path through the woods, and do not loiter by the way, or run, for you might fall and break the eggs."

"I will do just as you tell me," Red Riding-Hood promised.

SO she walked happily along the path, and into the deep woods. The birds sang above her head.

LITTLE RED RIDING-HOOD

ALL at once a little rabbit scampered out from a clump of ferns.

"Good-morning, Bunny," said Little Red Riding-Hood. But Bunny was frightened, and ran away.

LITTLE RED RIDING-HOOD

A LITTLE farther on, she met a wolf. Red Riding-Hood did not know what a wicked animal he was, so she was not afraid of him.

"Good-morning, Red Riding-Hood," said the wolf.

"Good-morning, Wolf," she replied.

"Where are you going so early?" he asked.

"I am going to grandmother's," said Little Red Riding-Hood.

THE wolf walked along with her. "Where does your grandmother live?" he asked,

"In the little cottage at the other side of the wood," answered Red Riding-Hood.

The wicked wolf thought to himself, "I will eat her up after a while, but first I will eat up the grandmother."

Then he said, "Why don't you pick some of these pretty flowers?"

LITTLE RED RIDING-HOOD

RED Riding - Hood looked at the bright flowers and thought, "I am sure Grannie would be pleased if I took her a bunch of fresh flowers. It is quite early and I shall have plenty of time to pick them." So she set her basket down, and wandered about, among the trees. Each time she picked a flower she saw a prettier one farther on.

LITTLE RED RIDING-HOOD

IN the meantime, the wolf went straight to the grandmother's cottage, and knocked at the door.

"Who is there?"

"Red Riding-Hood, bringing you butter and eggs."

"Pull the bobbin, and the latch will go up," said the old grandmother.

SO the wolf pulled the bobbin and opened the door. But when the grandmother saw his wicked face, she jumped out of bed and ran out the back door, dropping her night-cap as she ran.

LITTLE RED RIDING-HOOD

THE wolf snatched up the night-cap and put it on his ugly head, jumped into bed and covered himself with the bed-clothes.

VERY soon there came a knock at the door.

"Who is there?" called the wolf.

"It is Little Red Riding-Hood, grandmother dear. I have brought you some butter and eggs."

Then the wolf, trying to make his voice soft, like grandmother's called, "Pull the bobbin, and the latch will go up."

SO Little Red Riding-Hood pulled the bobbin and walked in. "Goodmorning, dear grandmother," she said, "How are you feeling today?"

"Very bad indeed, my dear," answered the wolf, trying to hide himself under the bed-clothes.

RED Riding-Hood drew nearer to the bed. "Grandmother," she said, "What very bright eyes you have!"

"The better to see you with, my dear," said the wolf.

"Grandmother, what great ears you have!"

"The better to hear you with, my child,"

"Grandmother, what great big teeth you have!" said Red Riding-Hood, who was beginning to get frightened.

"THE better to eat you with!" cried the wolf, and leaped out of bed; but he became entangled in the bed-clothes, and before he could reach Red Riding-Hood, she climbed right up the bed-post, over upon the old canopy top and sat there, all scrunched up against the wall, and knew she was safe.

THE wolf leaped about and tried to reach her. He looked so funny, because he was so very cross and angry, and he still had grandmother's cap on.

WHEN the wolf found he could not reach her, he got into bed again. It was very quiet in the little house for some time.

THEN the door opened, and in came a woodman, who had been chopping trees in the forest. Close behind him came the dear grandmother.

LITTLE RED RIDING-HOOD

THE wicked wolf sprang out of bed, and tried to run out the back door, but the woodman killed him, and gently lifted Little Red Riding-Hood from the top of the bed.

LITTLE RED RIDING-HOOD

HOW glad she was to be safe in grandmother's arms!

The woodman dragged the old wolf out into the deep woods. Then he came back, grandmother had put on her new dress, with a soft 'kerchief around her neck.

SHE smiled at the woodman and said, "You saved Red Riding-Hood's life and I am very grateful: so I am going into the village to live, in another little house which I have there, and I give to you this house in the woods."

"This house to me!" said the woodman, in great surprise. "How can I ever thank you? It is a wonderful thing, because I have no home."

"YOU have a home now," said grandmother, "And I gladly give it to you."

Very soon they started away, the woodman going with them till they were in sight of Red Riding-Hood's home; and there was dear mother coming to meet them.

LITTLE RED RIDING-HOOD

AND the next day grandmother had the nicest tea-party, so that all of Red Riding-Hood's little friends might come to see her, and tell her how happy they were that the wicked wolf was dead, and that Little Red Riding-Hood was safely home again.